DATE DUE

A Child's Good Night Book

Margaret Wise Brown

pictures by
Jean Charlot

📖 HarperCollins*Publishers*

Copyright © 1943, 1950 by Margaret Wise Brown
Copyright renewed 1978 by Roberta B. Rauch
First published by William R. Scott, Inc.
Printed in the U.S.A. All rights reserved.
New Edition, 1992
ISBN 0-06-021028-1. — ISBN 0-06-020752-3 (lib. bdg.)
Library of Congress Catalog Card Number 91-45340

Night is coming. Everything is going to sleep. The sun goes over to the

other side of the world. Lights turn
on in all the houses. It is dark.

All the little birds stop singing and flying and eating.
And they tuck their heads under their wings and go to sleep.

Sleepy birds.

The little fish in the darkened sea sleep with their eyes wide open.

Sleepy fish.

The sheep in the fields huddle together in a great warm blanket of wool. The lambs stop leaping, and the rams stop ramming, and the sheep stop *baaa*-ing, and they all go to sleep.

Sleepy sheep.

The wild monkeys
and the wild lions
and the wild mice
all close their eyes
in the forest.

Sleepy wild things.

The little sailboats
furl their sails and
are tied up at their
docks for the night.

Quiet sailboats.

And the cars and trucks and airplanes are all put in their houses—in dark garages and hangars. Their engines stop.

Quiet engines.

And the little kangaroos jump in their mothers' warm pouches and close their eyes.

Sleepy kangaroos.

The purring pussycats
blink their eyes.
Then their eyes close,
and they stop purring.

Sleepy pussycats.

The bunnies close their bright red eyes.

Sleepy bunnies.

The children stop thinking
and whistling and talking.
They say their prayers, get
under their covers, and go
to sleep.

Sleepy children.

Dear Father, hear and bless

Thy beasts and singing birds,

And guard with tenderness

Small things that have no words.